Where is the Pinky Ponk going?

Andrew Davenport

Once upon a time in the Night Garden...

The Pinky Ponk came to play.

Igglepiggle, iggle onk,
We're going to catch...

The Pinky Ponk!

One day Igglepiggle, Upsy Daisy,
the Tombliboos and Makka Pakka
went for a ride on the Pinky Ponk.

Somebody else went too.

Mi-mi-mi!

Do you know who it was?

The teeny tiny Pontipines, of course!

Ponk! Ponk! Ponk!

Where is the Pinky Ponk going?

Over Upsy Daisy's bed...

over Makka Pakka's house...

over the Tombliboo bush...

Ponk! Ponk! Ponk!

Where is the Pinky Ponk going?

Up and up...
and up.

Higher and higher...
and higher.

Into the branches
of a very tall tree.

Ponk! Ponk! Ponk!

Where is the Pinky Ponk going?

Up and up...
and up and up,
went everybody
in the Pinky Ponk.

Higher and higher...
and higher and higher,
right to the very top
of the tree.

And do you know what they saw?

Look at that.
A special thing. That is the bud
of the Olly-bolly-dob-dob flower.

Very rare indeed.

And look – it's beginning to open!

One flower,

two flowers,

three flowers,

four!

More... and more... and more... and more!

The Olly-bolly-dob-dob flower!

The Pinky Ponk took us all that way, just in time to see the Olly-bolly-dob-dob flower.

Isn't that a pip?

Once upon a time
in the Night Garden,

the Pinky Ponk took everybody
to see a special thing.

The Olly-bolly-dob-dob flower.
Thank you, Pinky Ponk.

Time to go to sleep everybody.

Go to sleep, Makka Pakka.

Go to sleep, Upsy Daisy.

Go to sleep, Pontipines.

Go to sleep, Tombliboos.
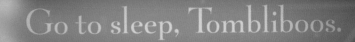

Go to sleep, Haahoos.

Go to sleep Ninky Nonk
and go to sleep, Pinky Ponk.
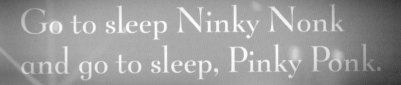

Wait a minute.
Somebody is not in bed!
Who's not in bed?
Igglepiggle is not in bed!

Don't worry, Igglepiggle...
it's time to go.